# NYLUND,

## THE SARCOGRAPHER

# NYLUND,
# THE SARCOGRAPHER

## JOYELLE MCSWEENEY

Tarpaulin Sky Press
Townshend, Vermont
2007

Nylund, the Sarcographer
© 2007 Joyelle McSweeney

First edition, October 2007.
ISBN: 978-0-9779019-4-4
Printed and bound in the USA.
Library of Congress Control Number: 2007920047

Cover and book design by Christian Peet.
Text is in Jenson. Titles are in Downcome and Nail Scratch, designed
by Eduardo Recife, Misprinted Type (Brazil).

Tarpaulin Sky Press
Townshend, Vermont
www.tarpaulinsky.com

*Nylund, the Sarcographer* is also available in a limited hand-bound
edition from Tarpaulin Sky Press.

For more information on Tarpaulin Sky Press perfect-bound and
hand-bound editions, as well as information regarding distribution,
personal orders, and catalogue requests, please visit our website at
www.tarpaulinsky.com.

# TABLE OF CONTENTS

# CHAPTER 1
## I'M A LUG

What else could I be as I walked down the street but a sarcographer of raining. I had to build a cask around it, built like itself. Tell me, where is Beauty Bread? goes the gag question. Save it for the Joy Page; I get it all the time. This time I did almost no hearing as I watched the puddles brim oddly like clavicles on the splayed street. The kits and cats waggled non-spayed pudenda. I was all wet. I bent like a spout and circled the building. Last week the cat burglar hid the diamonds in plain sight, enlacing the wrought iron railing. I read it in Crook Parade. Last month they hid the money in the cake. Now the evening is grinning like a combination lock. Now a stranger steps away from the stand, the green felfelt chair stumped down the glistery seement stair on the magazine face well, well, I was thinking of you nylons in the open window getting wet. The four legs kick one way like fangirls or a stutterframed weathercock. Fine rain we're having. You don't feel that way about it when it's your job. You don't even see the legs anymore just the gridded polymers hot from the mold. They got two densities throwing light on the damp interior. The blooming grey bank of the couch. If there's another world war just c'mon over with your bank where the hyssop grows. Giggling and combing each other's hair 'til the day. Look you got black roots, negligee, a cigarette hanging from your mouth like a streetsign slumped on its post and pointing wanly at the gravel shoulder. Your skin will be grey in the time lapse of smokophilia but now it's beach-weed yellow, your hair white like a rich baby's. There's a margin of aristocracy where your hair and shoulders meet. C'mon tumble down the ladder, baby. Double up in the craft I've converted from house to boat.

It mopes. It doesn't like its job as a coffin.

But you knocked me out, heiress. Rope a dope.

We wanted to get rich by writing one-liners for the joke page in Reader's Digest you read when the school nurse took you to County to get your tetanus. Laff Parade. Nothing more natural than the way that ripped can bit your ankle. Or the beahavior mags with Goofus and Gallant strutting down the street in matching cornball shirts. We could do that. If only we could twin our behavior to oppositely arrive.

One of them turned into a store.

By which I mean: twin of mine. The green light streaming off the tackle. The pinstripe of the buttery lines. Paw off on a drunk. The drunk tank like a houseboat. We could go and bid him out or we could tow the line. You could get it for a kiss and a pull off the whiskey beetle. Nobody bleeved we were twins who didn't know Maw. Later our faces were red, both in the same way, and nobody could forget it.

Your skinned knee.

The table cloth straight as a diagram.

*Sit on the floor, dogs.*

*No not there on the good linoleum.*

I'm wet to my cuffs. I'm feeling my grommets. I'm feeling my age today. My wingtips can't breathe in all this moisture. I'm feeling the black ribs of the lamppost where I grubbed and felt her up. I'm feeling the tooth of the lancet where the stitch went in, last week. Then the tight band around it, then the trouser loosed over the leg. Striped like a road like a streak of gelding going south. Flood down the leg and into the other lappings that tide us all into destination. It's relative, can't be helped. I'm feeling the grain where I grubbed the mast and the mess where I embarrassed the masthead.

# CHAPTER 2
## WHAT DO YOU WANT

The editor's mouth sagged like a dog losing at poker there was a lake of mien there was a lake of ink he was trying to break the habit of falling into but failing chewed on pens. He was trying like the state of Minnesota in frame after frame and he was a failing bucket. The stripes ran up his chest and there was a chain stuffed in his pocket. It ticked through his well-stocked barrel belly like a baby mewling in a well floating in a walled-up sea. Drip. How long till this goes under. "Did you think you could pull one over on me?"

"Nuh-no sir I did not."

I was aproned, I had a push cart of letters in brown envelopes. I was erratic, I would keep half stacked in my stash in the basement and I tried to place my hand on one and read its innards like an ancient roman. I would never open them which would be breaking the federal law. I was trying to be a sarcographer of reading. I'd trafficked in other telepathies. But when one too many shoebuckles popped open on my watch and caused a lady to prettily lean I gave it up. Jesus was watching and had enough of my sidewalk casuistry.

Nuh-no sir I did not think.

Now I admit I'd dreamed of the profit. In Kazakhstan I dream a snowy pasha with a wool fringe and a rug and a brilliant carnadine vest sewn with mirrors I never take off. The mirrors stand for peacocks' eyes. The peacocks stand for the pretty rumors which spread and lifted me from a lowly shepherd to the head of Kazakhstry and that's why I rule the steppes with the golden llama I stole from the pen.

Instead, I'd pad on cracked soles that creeped and bugged the editors hunched over their dailies. Blue pen-

cils hushed silently around. Rats scribbled in the walls
I heard the second novel being written around this one
and I wondered about their nests. I left one letter a week
by the door to the janitor's closet where I felt sure they'd
find it.

Wednesday was my night for thinking about the rats.

They were writing it even now.

Writing under and over the one I'm listening to.

I loved the basement. The pressroom I wasn't allowed in,
the incredible pressures of the paper's belts. They had a
special squad of men for that who didn't like me for my
girly insoles and my insolence, a haircut they observed
with my head down. They read my tealeaves in the part
of my cowlicked. In the curls that tossed like the sea or
a colicky baby: wracked. They teased a stutter out of me,
my hands in my pockets. It was just a charade. It was just
practice. They weren't even clenched there. The stutter
was amplification.

My hands were soft as steamed envelopes

Which I never. Not in the office. Nor ever took any tea.

Now the editor asks. "What did you want with them anyway? The press is an organ of society. We have to hear our readers."

Believe me, I see. I'm all for better hearing. I'm all for re-using the spools at the core of threads and the eyes of needles. So much of our resources are being put to waste, and if it's not the Russians it's the gangsters get the better of us. We opened a rank can with Prohibition.

"Nylund," he says, "you're a lonely man. Don't you have a wife—or a mother!—someone to look after you?"

"Nuh-neither," I say.

No, sir, I have a twin.

# CHAPTER 3
## OVERHAUL

The sea snake struggles through the concrete, stuck; its sea has paralyzed around it. It exists in hemi-arabesques; half, by half, by half and never progresses or seizes up out of this moment. The five brown towers rise like sepals around this unpromising bed. Windows open sideways high as the grimy cloud ceiling; here and there a woman rests her elbows on the metal sill and contemplates this monster geometry, which is colossal and exact. Any child's hand can grasp it: The sky baffles the ground. The sky is a ground for what hieroglyphs may be tossed there by the vagaries of the human candle, police lights, premieres. The woman turns the light on herself like the spray of a shower. She slowly turns her pretty head. Some stories up, the flat curl of the tire plant is pinned in place with the shrewd dart of a jet.

Any child's hand can manage the way the buildings scratch at the cloud-jerkin as at an itchy back. This is a sleep without invective but with tiny discrete infections wallowing in shores, in the pedal antipodes, the feet poking free of the quilt as if to touch down into another life, there to fasten on the cloudy doublet, grip the scimitar and ride off after the lady whose persimmon trousers sink in the far distance. Or the hand thrown up on the cool pillow half open, where a tight scroll or trombone slide or revolver might fit. At the morning alarm the body jackknifes, slaps hand to ankle, swivels its bit into the life that was nowhere in the night's divers collection.

\*

Nylund in his bed. The sheets' sarcography. Last evening's events battening him like something to be regretted. Why? How he passed the dim alley of silhouettes. How he witnessed the usual congresses of hands and hips and throats. Then a gathering of nightshade blue uniforms by the stoop of the brown midblock building. On the lintel, numbers had fallen away and left pale eidolons, each empty space punched with a nailhole which asterisked the building. Across the street, he placed his hand on a railing caging the base of a tree and drew the leafy blackness around him. Silverbuttoned and then trenchcoated men emitted from the house. They shut themselves into cars and were drawn away. And then replenished and sped up the stairs on the gust of an ascending angel. The cop on guard turned his flashlight on Nylund's face. Hey moonface, over here.

Nylund breathed for a moment before willing himself to separate from the shadow which put its hands on his cheeks and kissed his face. His upper body went stiff and paperlight as he rose and fell across the street. The cop just watched him approach, his features thick as a slow schooner turning around.

"Whatch you doin out here tonight, paper-moon?"

Nylund could think of no answer. Practicing sarcography.

"Well look there's been some bad business in this house. I don't suppose you know nothin about it?"

"Nuh-no. What kind of business?"

"The kind of business that's none of your business, if you don't know nothin about it."

"I was just wuh-walking by, really." In moments of stress, Nylund's chin made a motion like a typewriter when someone's punched return. It jerked right, then jerked left to its angle of incidence. The cop's eyes narrowed, and stayed narrow as his mouth relaxed.

"Alright buddy. I'll take your word for it. But I'm taking down your name. I don't like how you were watching this house. You should keep moving on a night like this."

Nylund gave his name and the address of the newspaper where he no longer worked to the policeman, who recorded same with a stubby pencil on a ludicrously small pad. Nylund turned and took a few steps away. It was as difficult to turn his back on this lit up house as to turn his back, permanently, on the sun. The lamplight placed firm hands on his shoulders. But he kept walking, with effort, away from the scene now still as fruit on a table, whores on a lawn, away from the house of bad business.

*

Three blocks away Nylund stopped. He was huge and furious, his carapace big as the sky's. He shoved his feelers in his mouth then vomited out a thick beam of blackness. *On a night like this you should keep moving!* he screamed at the windows. He shoved himself through the walls. On the second floor, he scuttled up the sill to the wainscoting. He trundled along; dropped down amid the boxes in the pantry, touching every grain of rice. *On a night like this!* He skittered the floors. When light fell on him from any source, he moved faster and more efficiently. Like information, he melted through the wall. Appeared to screams on the table, on the open book littered with black unhygienic-looking specks. He whispered into the hand of a baby asleep in a crib, and the baby breathed in response. He scaled its pink cheek, crawled across its pink wooly hat, with difficulty. *YOU SHOULD KEEP MOVING* he bellowed to each limb as it sunk in to the resiny stuff, finally clambering off the hot dome and onto the cool rail of the crib, then over the wallpaper's humid cranial ridges. He reached the firescape like a railroad of diamonds, he arrived back at his own shoes again. They held his human feet. He was wet and panting. On a night like this.

# CHAPTER 4
## LIKE A PELICAN
## IN THE WILDERNESS

Nylund slumped from his bed to the lion-colored table that had been gnawed on all its edges by a gang of delinquent toddlers. Surprisingly steady, it held the weight of his body as he dropped himself onto his ladderback. His jaw was aching. Someway he slept. His left wrist felt absent. He tried to clutch at the edge of the table but his bum hand sunned itself like an upturned rowboat in the shallow of his lap.

Sun was pouring through the window as battery and flappable as the yellow curtains copying its moves. The rivals pushed playfully at each other then turned their gaze on Nylund. They held their fists for now at waist level. He dropped his chin away. He stood up and turned to the

graywhite laminate countertop who was specked opti-
mistically with gold foil. He lay a damp hand against the
cool of it. It was lukewarm. He flipped a decisive switch
and performed his morning routine, and soon pleasantly
burning olfactory cities and earthy plains were sprouting
around his ears as he sat back down at the table, and soon
a soily cup of coffee warmed his palm and a scorched
piece of toast lay on its aqua plate, the day's first bland yet
indisputable production.

The knowledge of the bad business appeared like a knot
of emerald ribbon which he traced with his mind's eye.
It wound like scarves or twitched like cartoon snakes
through her locked apartment. Plush and level-headed,
it stopped to run its tongue and fingers over the raised
velvet pampas of the just-for-show couch this girl had
made her everyday bed. But it didn't find her there. The
couch opened like a conchshell opposite a huge wall mirror flanged in flamelike tongues. But she wasn't in the
mirror. She wasn't in the fireplace with the ornate screen.
It turned and fingered the lemon-colored sheets folded
neatly on a nearby chair, it stewed over to the closet where
it nuzzled the ivory kidskin gloves the worn brown and
black purses and dead-feathered hats fit to the crown of

the head which coated the upper shelves above the rack of dresses. But she was not hiding amid the dresses nor folded amid the coats. It sighed, it grew in strength, it picked itself up and steered itself over to the last door behind which a bath was running. There it found her, seated before an oval mirror, her brown hair wound in a towel, her slim wrists tied prettily behind her.

Her slim wrists tied prettily behind her and to the gold-plated wire of the icecream parlor chair which formed an inverted tulip at the small of her back. She was naked and her whole body flushed red, and in the mirror her head was bowed and her eyes closed demurely. The clean white gag parted her bright red lips and tied at the nape of her neck above a sweet curl of damp brown hair. She looked sunburnt, but how does a girl in this city get sunburnt on every inch of her body. In November. She might have been a glamour girl, swept away and back on the tide of personal whim. The apartment though cheap suggested it: the kind of glamor for which dispensability is an article of faith.

The wetness of the night had ensured no fire started before the cops had arrived. The first cop in had stopped the water running and he and every cop subsequent had stepped in the puddles and tracked wet evidential footprints over the passive pink carpet before they had realized what they were doing. The second cop in had searched out the source of the gas, a cracked pink enamel range in the cramped galley kitchen, and dialed the poison closed. The windows were thrown open. There the green knot tightened to a pinpoint and disappeared.

The muddy carpet had looked like the Seine at night, streaked with pink muddy light from the sky, or like a rosebank after heavy rain, or the aftermath of an allmale garden party: kinky. Nylund had walked by the large department stores and seen small nodes of women emerge wearing hats as if guiding a flotilla of flowery islands down a river of Nereids' hair. The effect proved artificial like a Victorian night charade, each woman's head gleaming with a prow-shaped coif which bore up the sheaf of flowers. It was afternoon as Nylund watched this incredible current emerge and pull to a thread in both directions down the sidewalk, then thin out completely and disappear.

Now he broke the invisible still present cordon of slim

grasping hands and delicate suit sleeves and swinging purses and stepped into the whirr of the gold and glass revolving and into the department store. He pushed through a dark wood foyer just a few feet in depth and stood up on the gleaming tidal floor of an incredible gallery which climbed many stories in the air. His pores glutted with perfumes, producing an earthbound vertigo; gold gratings winged up the corner columns, the open floor swam with booths and counters and white and black smocked lady clerks and men in alarmingly narrow fitted jackets, as if these men could themselves bed down in the thin drawers holding luxury ties or slot through the credit card devices. With frequency, imitation fir pinnacles scrolled up and over the laneways and climbed for the ivory ceiling which seemed it would evaporate at any minute to reveal the grey heavens of offices above. Light leapt from gold ball to security mirror to perfume flask to eyeglass frame. The scene dazzled for the time it took one pump of blood to reach the heart and be returned, and then it thickened, matted up on the membrane and could not be admitted. Nylund breathed through his teeth.

The buttons glared from the double-breasted elevator plaque as if annoyed to be in such close quarters with

Nylund. He chose the highest-numbered one and was surprised to find himself not in the business offices but in the low ceilinged maidquarters cum global holiday bazaar. Pink-haired and nose-ringed kids were putting the finishing touches on the various displays, each dedicated to a chic destination spot. A chubby boy in a too-tight mesh tank top and curly hair shaped into horns was fluffing the tufts of a bearskin rug in a replica ice hotel representing far northern Sweden. An Asian woman in striped stockings was applying gluey bubbles to the cocktails being served on an Emirates Air flight by stewardesses in peach veils affixed to baby-aspirin pillboxes. Nylund stepped around half-unpacked boxes, ladder rungs and contorted, laboring art-school bodies till he reached the apparent zenith of this global tour, a view of Rio de Janiero complete with the tourist office Jesus, his arms draped with bags adorned with the logo of the department store. Tiny toy airplanes climbed fishing wires in the air; one thought of King Kong. As Nylund stood contemplating this, a girl with a ropy assortment of carrot-colored braids approached him.

"Hold this," she said, plunking a purple and gold trimmed treasure chest in his arms, and bending down to straighten the thread-thin thong worn by a volley ball player on the shoe-sized beach.

"Wha-what's this for?" Startled, the girl jerked and peered up at him through brown cateyed glasses with brown cateyes.

"You don't work here? You shouldn't be up here yet," she said, taking the treasure out of his arms. It had been much lighter than it looked, but now without it his arms felt weightless, as if they would rise up toward the ceiling like a zombie's.

"It's to enter a drawing for a trip. They're going to have one at every station."

Nylund could think of nothing at all to say.

"Look, you're not supposed to be up here, but if you want to enter your name I'll stick it in when we've got it all ready." She handed him a piece of white paper, he filled in his name and the phone number of the office where Armenian Rose worked the front desk. She'd take a message for him.

"Nylund" she said, looking at the paper. "You're a dentist?"

"Nuh-no. I want a job here."

"Oh", she said. "The seasonal office is a street door downstairs, and you have to get here at 6 AM and line up. That's what we all did. We're from Stray Arts."

"Oh."

"Uh-oh is right. You want to go get a cigarette?" The girl clapped her hands together to knock the dust or plastic snow from them. A stray green ribbon coiled around her ankle and across the parquet floor. This made Nylund feel sad. He had forgotten something.

"No. I've got to be going now."

"Ok, Nylund. I'm Lauren. See you around, maybe, if you get that job." She stuck out her hand.

"Suh-see you around."

The ride down is always faster than the ride up, thought Nylund, lurching hellwards on rickety wooden escalators, catching glimpses of shoes and suits and luggage and his own reflection stretched taffy thin in the smoked disconcerting mirrors. On every floor, people clumped and bent and looked for each other frantically like the inmates of some refugee processing center on some wartorn frontier. He slid down to streetlevel and found himself out in the dusk. The concrete, the grey sky, the wreath and wraithlike shape of his breath, it was all degrees of the same element. The cold moved up through his shoes and in through his jaw. Looney medical advice assembled itself before his mind's eye. *One lump or two?* For toothache, tie a dinner napkin under the gullet. For a fistfight, don a beefsteak mask. The former to ward off enemies. The latter, shiny, dull, to invite another slug.

His thoughts made long diagonals like a pushbroom, clearing the sidewalk. He slid around in the widening air. He climbed to platforms, he slid horizontally, he sunk lower into tunnels, he rode up again to the overground. He came out into the blue night of his own neighborhood. Under the hat of the floorlamp, he watched a television program about a teen in Ingushetia with a tongue the size of an American football lolling out his mouth. Like a pelican in the wilderness, he could cluck food down around it, but they took him to Moscow and cut it down. Now his mouth can close, albeit in a continually surprised 'o'. He has a normal life, works in a factory planing boards.

When asked about his new life, he says: "Well, it could pay a bit more."

It could pay a bit more, Nylund thought. On the screen, cans of pink matter balanced on velvet pillowed pedestals caressed by a sultry white cat. In the next ad, dogs leapt through brightly colored hoops and tottered two-footed in shiny swallow-tailed jackets. A man asked his dog for the recipe for baked beans. A man threw his dog a turkey sausage. Suburbanites and animals frolicked animatedly on the edges of his consciousness while a green sward shaped itself into a thoroughfare that ran right through him to the back of his skull like the tongue in his own throat and he was to tumble right down it to the neighborhood of bad business. But he felt like resisting for tonight. He knew it would be there waiting for him when he woke up.

I'm going to be alright, Nylund thought. And I'm going to be right like a pelican in the wilderness.

# CHAPTER 5

The boulders were small-town prehistoric. Or like reduced for sale. They rose only so far and the dropoff was only so deep, which made the place dangerous. The dangerousness made for a tank of boys. Girls would come in twos or threes in Woolworth swimsuits or tanktops the color of candy, stay a few hours, and leave. But Daisy went alone with only him and she wore a red bandanna tied around her flat chest and they carried towels he had taken from a line and worried someone would recognize. It was hard to relax. When he closed his eyes into the sun he could see the green in it. Then open them to a world burnt white or black with Daisy gone or back her red lips stained with Koolaid red soda.

Opposite was a ropeswing one of the boys had burnt off while sitting on its tire base. He had plunked into the water. End of show. Another time two brothers had flown off the wall in a shopping cart and into the quarry. They started out screaming but went down quiet as if in surprise. One wrenched his ankle doing it and he couldn't bear his own weight when he climbed out. The other had blood running in thin pink drizzles over the white of his thigh. They both settled dazed on a log until they could figure how to get home on their bikes. Then some big boy threw one of their bikes in the quarry and one brother started to cry. That one had to keep at the back of things, when he came back.

Daisy and he sat apart. She liked to get hot and then jump in the water and then jump out and let her hair dry again. Daisy liked to be this or that, just two things. With the two of them, that was easy. Back at the house their eyes were burnt out from the sunlight and even at noon the house seemed sunk in. Darkness seeped out from under the corroding chairs and rayed from the warped doors. Mold grew blackly under the window sills as if to say: *you're making me do this.* Daisy and him would climb in the tub and just lay across the cold back of it, not talking. Or one of them outside tried to guess at the position of the other behind the olive green curtain. It was scary to watch the hand you couldn't see suddenly press through the vinyl. It was great to be reached for, to be tickled and seized by that strange vinyl hand.

At night their cousins came home in their uniforms and sat in a tent of kitchen light over hamburgers and then he and Daisy went outside. The pines whipped around green black as if unleashed, finally animated, and you could shout in the woods with noone around to hear you but yourself over—echoey. Playing lost, they fell into each other's blue grey arms natural as into your own ghost. Late at night they snuck back in and watched the TV silently while the one cousin was still out and the other asleep. They let it flicker over them till they were asleep. It was like sleeping underwater.

Of them, the cousins had been heard to say: *Those two just watch TV all day.*

For him, school mixed in certainties with mysteries; he could never pick out the rule. She was or she wasn't in class, graphing, or serving a volleyball or studying the cakey contour map with dull eyes. She was or she wasn't in the principal's office with the door closed. She would or she wouldn't carry free lunches of even-toned islands injection-molded into plastic compartments, alongside him. She would or she wouldn't talk. Talking to Daisy made a little dug-out hull of quiet in the steady roar of the schoolday, the size of her two cupped hands. Where were *his* hands, building it? Out of school, the plastic ring or the found key or the dime fell into the bed of dry pin-needles and was pretty much gone. The rag doll set up against a pine trunk was there the next night, and the next night, and the next, its faithful dress and features slowly wiped away by weather 'til it turned into trash. At school, the expensive cans of soda and snacks pressed up in their dozens in the coiled machine fell away and banged like angels against its invisible floor. Sometimes two fell out by accident or you would hear the machine was broken and kids clotted around it till the display was emptied or the principal walked past. Some knowledge was dispensed or communicated, usually contaminated or corrupted as it passed through many hands. When your ears burned that was someone talking. When you felt a chill on your neck that was the angel of death passing you by. He always felt that. The one angel pacing and passing him by.

# CHAPTER 6:
## ARMENIAN ROSE

All the doors in this building were of a prisonblanket grey which discouraged penetration while inviting desecration, and 1E's was no exception, except that its bland expanse was free of incised threats, its doorstep uncluttered by lurid circulars and the toothy lids of softdrinks. A frosted card in neat black brackets spared a single word for passersby in a reversed, inward script that floated ethereally. The vision of this word had a strange effect on Nylund. It communicated directly with his brainstem; his motor skills balked; and as he paused to contemplate the white, continual crispness of this namecard, that vaunted ichor gathered around him like a kiss from a fox-stoled stepmother or the first semester of an epileptic fit: *Rose.*

A strange effect, yes, but he would swear to it, if asked. The occasion did not present itself.

Rose was a receptionist at a dentist's office four blocks west. The office saw few patients. Those few who did drop in had been doing so faithfully for decades, and came wrapped in so many furs one would think they were trying out a second species for the presumptive afterlife, or else clad in such sedate grey suits they'd be indistinguishable from the sidewalk if they chose to lie down. The dentist had been set up in business by a moderately wealthy wife, whom he had outlived; now he kept the office up in a belated surge of fidelity. His wife had taken special care with the decor. Rose's desk was made of heavy dark wood and was surmounted by a clock in which a white, leonine face sat calmly in a cage of mirrory gold. Behind the desk, a huge mural in purples, greens, winereds and blues stretched across an entire wall. It featured the mountainrange shoulders and cable-tendon neck of a man whose head lolled lazily to one side, his eyes closed, his mouth slightly parted. A thick band was pressed amid his antic curls. So heavy were his features and visible limbs that he seemed at once carved of marble and the sea. His bare arms were slightly raised as if he were about to embrace the room: Eames chairs, Rose and all.

This unpromising young man, Rose would inform you, was Morpheus.

Nearly weightless herself, Rose balanced at the desk like her namesake. She wore a starched white uniform with three-quarter sleeves and a Chinese collar. Her white hair hung smooth as a knifeblade to her shoulders and showed two sharp points below her chin. Her skin was wrinkled and freckled to a beachy evenness, and she studied her petitioners with sea green eyes. She kept one slim hand poised at all times on the huge polished black receiver.

"Nylund, it's not cocktail hour yet."

Nylund looked at the clock at Rose's elbow. Five minutes to five. He shrugged and sat down in one of the Eames chairs.

"Cuh-couldn't wait to see you, Rose."

"A gentleman is never early, Nylund. Time you learned that." Nylund thought he saw a slight smile at the corner of Rose's scarlet mouth, like the curling of an autumn leaf, but, looking closer, he didn't. "There are few gentlemen left, they are a dying species, but all the more reason to study their language and their habits."

Though Nylund often rose to the occasion with Rose, his record was regrettably uneven. He had already contributed one quip this time out, and could think of nothing else to say. He shrugged again. Rose didn't 'tsk' verbally, but he could see that familiar look ride across her face.

"I'm ready to go now, Nylund."

He rose and came around the corner of Rose's desk and offered her his arm. She held on with one hand as she rose incredibly slowly to a standing position. It was only when rising or settling herself that Rose resembled the old lady she was, and Nylund couldn't help being enthralled by this delicacy. He reached down her plain, chic trenchcoat from the treestand and helped her into it. She belted it firmly and settled a black beret on her head. There were no papers to straighten or coworkers to salute on the way out, as the office was entirely empty. He followed her out to the elevator.

On the ground floor, he pushed the gate aside and led Rose out into the sleety sidewalk. He held open her extraordinary antique umbrella which had already lasted three decades and Rose glided along under it like the figurehead of her own ship. They made slow progress across the four blocks, the poppy-colored "don't walk" signs blaring at inconvenient moments, the gutters running thickly and animatedly like teams of overexcited boys. At their building, Nylund twirled the umbrella slowly to glide the rain off, and handed its bent handle to Rose. They walked down the tiled and grimly greenish halls in a more contemplative silence, as if coming under this roof for the first time. When she had her door open, Rose turned to face him. She was thin as a tine and came up to his sternum.

"Goodnight now, Nylund," she said. Not waiting for an answer, she slid in the door and pulled it shut behind her. Caught up short, Nylund found himself face to face with her name on the door, felt the sleepy, somewhat nauseating arms of scent close around him. He shook them off and walked hurriedly down the hall towards the elevator. Then, having pushed the call button, he turned and walked rapidly down the hall and out and back into the street.

# CHAPTER 7

It was ninepins and they all fell open. It was nine pines on a hilltop, and the thousands of pines around them. The network, the extended family. He was winging away from them on the burst blades of a helicopter. He was cruising into them with his grown sons in tow, and with his ungrown sons, and with his children coiled in his belly. He was the head of sports, an important man. He had his children in his mouth. He crawled over the snow slope with his shaggy profits beard and his four tawny feet spreading out over the snow. He lowed. He had his children in his mouth. His voice came out around them and there was a space for them in it shaped like themselves. They were the holes in the prophecy and he buried them in caves, he buried them under the pyramid. Then he returned like dogs to the pyramids and dug them up

34

again. Then he returned like weather to the pyramids and blew them down. He was in an ivory cage that stank like mottled meat, it was his own cage, and the cage of his own mouth. He paced in it; he revolved and gagged. He revoluted. The keeper came with meat on a hook and wavered it near his mouth. He battled at it. He drank it down keeper and all and felt him punching in his gut. He snaked like a root down his mouth, then he stuck his Popeye arm out and punched him on the snout. He gagged, he fell out, covered in a caul. He cut the caul off him with the jagged roof of the mouth of the tin can. *Ow. It bit my ankle.* He turned to her. She was grown up and not a child. She had the long thin royal green sash tied around her ankle. *Ow*, she said. *Nylund, ow.* She smiled and said it. Her lips pulled and showed her teeth like candy even in a row. He wanted to press one out. He wanted to keep it. She spat one out. He got to his knees and searched for it in the virulent grass that was spreading across the basement. Long seams of mold zagged down the wall and split open. He took her hand and stepped out. He took her hand and led her out. He turned around, and every time she was there. He turned around, and her hair was growing. It grew around his ankles 'til he wasn't holding her hair but he was riding on it like a wave. He rose up past the top of the pines and he opened his mouth. *Your hair is growing!* he said to her. *Speak for yourself* she said. She held her fingers up to frame the moon and she turned it on him; and he could see his face in it and a long net of hair hanging to either side. There were bits of garbage and food and leaves in it and there were some little mice hanging by their necks. His long hair that used to be pretty. He looked at her and his face fell down. *Someone is crying* he said to her. She also said. She leaned over and touched her lips to his. They breathed while the water washed over them. Then their hair grew over them and she slapped his face.

# CHAPTER 8
## LABRAT

Why Nylund could spare sarcography for the lifestyle of the rich was a frustration to him and he blamed it on TV. While he thought of that teen in Ingushetia kissing, kissing himself to sleep. Air kisses. While he saw himself in undertaker's gear opening the front door like a cakey butler. The gravel driveway curved away like a uterus and the Mister and the Misssus were born through the threshold and into the house.

On TV, Nylund took the coats and put them away. In one corner of the coat closet the woman stirred. She was bound in sheets like a mummy or a costume party. Her brown hair was neatly parted and you could see her white part and the top of her white powdery forehead as she shivered a little and moaned. Leaning his head in through the wool shoulders he put his mouth to where her ear should be. *Steady,* he said. He stepped back and shut the door. He ran a hand over his own flat wing of grey hair and turned and made for the study where the Mister and the Missus were looking about themselves with mouths set and with eyes round in amazement as if they had happened on a body and were not just coming home.

*Well, Nylund, anything to report since we've been gone?* The Mister turned to him expectantly with hands clasped before him.

*Nothing in particular, sir,* Nylund responded, smooth as the Grey Ghost pulling off to the garage.

*Really, Nylund. Well I guess it's not surprising but we have been off the map and back again, subdued a rather nasty uprising and endured some revolting food. We make it all the way back round the horn to learn there's nothing new?*

*Sir.* With analog slowness, a roguish twinkle leapt from Nylund's eye to the Missus to the Mister and back to Nylund.

*Alright then, Nylund. Look we've these sacks of saffron and other spices.* The Mister and Missus began tugging from out of their clothing and about their feet enough stuffed sandbag-looking things to protect a town and placed them in Nylund's bent arms. The heap reached past the doorjamb, heavy as an ocean. *Lock them up in the larder for now until we work out who needs to be bought off.*

*Very good, sir.* Nylund turned and made for the door, preparing to bend his knees for the jamb, when the Missus stopped him.

*Oh, and Nylund, here are quantities of pearl.* His hands were full; she slid them one by one into his coat pockets. One by one by one by one. And although he could not feel their coolness he could feel them slide against the slick stuff of his linings.

\*

At work, Nylund wore a long blue coat which suited him, as if they were performing some scientific experiment in the freightelevators and backstairways and lower floors of the department store. Up and down invisibly, like worker

**39**

bees or cells. His Superior wore a narrow dark suit from which a gold flower burst improbably about the chest. He wore a disk of glass over one eye socket. His hair was slicked black and severely down. You couldn't look at him directly; he was always endeavoring to profile in front of you or turn at best to you a dancer's fifth position. If you looked at him from a tight enough angle he disappeared completely into the felicity of the air which was close in all the backstories of the building in which they worked. The man was light. "Liiiight, Nyluuund!" he would say, as if the utterance gave him the power to lift off the ground and arrange a sample plate on the top shelf of a china closet, as he was presently doing.

Nylund and he were in Home Furnishings, that was their site and their line, which was ironic, as Nylund's own home resembled a shipwreck, and it was impossible to imagine the Superior in any type of homesetting, or indeed outside the store. The Superior had an eye for detail, dust on the chandelier that needed evacuating or the foil unwrapping from a piece of chocolate in the little dish modeling a pedestal table. "Detaaaails, Nyluuund!" He was severe and keen as a bee.

The Superior sent Nylund into the building's receiving bays where he met large and small men working slowly or quickly. It was in nobody's best interest to work too efficiently but you could never tell when they were keeping track; other men thought it was self-respect to do the job as best you could, quick as you could. Nylund would go down with a green slip of paper on which the Superior had scratched in elaborate wings and downdrafts the name and color of whatever piece of furniture he required for the showroom; the man whose hand he placed it into would take this archaically unreadable glyph and turn to Nylund sad eyes which looked deeper and deeper down the archipelago of Nylund's interior to the smallest pea-shaped island in the chain. When the man's gaze had reached that far and could go no further, it was Nylund's cue to sigh, then shrug. Then the man would withdraw and sigh as well and find the console or ottoman or wing-chair that met as closely as possible whatever description their best efforts could derive from this inky vein.

Nylund was never sure if they guessed correctly but the Superior operated on such another cloud that he swept up whatever item was delivered to him and incorporated it into the display dais. He was currently recovering from a bout of eclecticism which had left him spent and nervous, though the handiwork of the illness was everywhere: three pale blond Swedish chairs dined with a plump velvet bound and betassled beauty at a slender table in the breakfast lounge. In the baby suite, a scary carousel horse lunged threateningly at a rocking chair while pulling in its wake the beveled bones of a prim white crib.

The Superior was a genius.

*

Nylund had the walk of the manor at night. He had a ring of keys like the chains of the dead he rattled to keep the chambermaids in their quarters. With more care a silent descent could be managed as the thick runner muffled footfalls. For the first night he was content to sit up in his room and imagine the steps he had not yet taken sinking into that nap. All the steps he had taken since taking the job, all the steps he had yet to take, stuffed into the deep red.

On the second night he decided to bestir himself and with each step he took down the main stair and toward the coat closet the thrill rose higher and higher in his body. When he reached the closet door, wider than you'd see in any smaller house, he stalled just for the pleasure of it. He could see in the dark. Light leapt in and out of his sprung pupils, dilettanted on his temples then out the tall windows to touch the silvery tips of the pines which dipped their heads fetchingly and threw their limbs out in all directions. Then he opened the door and sunk his hands into the fabric of the coats until he pushed through and felt the shape of her body behind them. With one hand on her he shouldered the coats aside and gathered her into his arms; the delightful shiver of that contact! The he folded her out of the closet, hoisted her lightly onto his shoulder, and began the long climb up to his quarters.

Gaslight filled his room as he opened the door and set her onto his bed. She fell back, and her head slipped lightly free of the sheets that wrapped her. The white flesh of her forehead caught the light and began to flush golden. Her dark ringlets hung away from her, her dark lashes matted thick, and her mouth fell slightly open to reveal the rim of her bottom teeth just above where her lips were reddening. He watched her as the blood came into her, as her chest began to rise slowly, as breath came thinly through that lovely parting. Soon she appeared to be asleep.

*

Nylund arrived at work one morning to find the Superior's face drawn to a point. It was like a knife turned on you if it was turned right on you you couldn't see it. The Superior's pointy posterior was deposited in an uncomfortable salmon velvet chair and his limbs were bent around him. He was thinking.

"What Furnishings needs, Nylund..."

Nylund waited for the predicate.

"What Furnishings needs, Nyluuund... is a plot!"

Nylund started.

"While I was on my way to work Nyluuund,"—so he didn't live here at the store—"I was quite annoyed watching a young man with his feet up on the seat across from him.

Well they're not ottomans, Nyluund! So I was sitting there wondering what star of ill breeding this young man was born under, when I realized I was staring at the tabloid that he held open. And what do you think it said?"

Nylund offered no guess.

"It said 'VANITY MURDER,' Nylund! So of course I was curious. I won't pretend I'm not guilty of that particular sin! When I reached the station, I picked one up, what do you think, Nylund? It's a vanity table, Nylund! A woman was murdered last week at her vanity table! Tied to it! Gassed!"

Although he had not moved, the Superior was shrieking. Nylund had no idea what would be the next word or pitch out of his mouth so he hovered there, his knees slightly bent.

"So, Nylund, it occurred to me, that many, many murders happen like that. In the household. In the home."

"Not a very Chr-Chr-Christmassy theme, sir."

"Oh, pffft!" The Superior said, turning his face away to spit out Nylund's thought. "Stores up and down this island have Christmassy themes this month. We're going to be the only one with the theme of 'Household Murders.'"

Nylund felt, he always felt, that resistance was futile.

# CHAPTER 9

When I was a child she was a child always right in front of me in a yellow sundress with orange and pink that softened and grew more sincerely botanical all over her as she grew up through it, her sharp knees poking out and her arms bent up around her head to fit in the frame. But when I grew up too I saw her only sideways, then through the few hazy centimeters between my eye and glasses. Daisy putting on ugly orange lipstick in the flip-down mirror of Big Cousin's car, and then pulling out the crumped map from under her and blotting it, leaving loud orange kissmarks across the faded flanks of the tristate. When she was driving it was the day that got the full view of her, and her hair all winging out around her in scrolling downdrafts and letters that were ugly and beautiful like child's play. Then I would look forward too at the road and wonder what it was seeing of me through the glass. Daisy and me had the same curls and my hair could be long—it could snarl up into pagodas or ziggurats or be soaped up into shark fins and maybe the road was right now looking at me and trying to see the way ground water would leave it for estuaries and runoffs or maybe read its own future, its own veined self splitting over the scuttling back horizon.

This was when Big Cousin had the night shift and would sleep drunk through the day. At first we'd try all manner of stealth, rolling the car down the lawn to the street before starting it, but the morning Daisy threw a coffee cup at the exhaust hood over the stove and the impact crashed a fry pan to the floor, and there was no response from Big Cousin's room, was the day she marched out there in her plastic shoes and started the car right outside his window. I slid into the seat next to her and we drove out side by side along the diamondflecked, morning-lit lanes of truancy.

*I need some coffee.*

*You threw yours at the wall!*

*That's what I mean, Nylund. I need some coffee.*

*Don't act so grownup.*

*Who's driving?*

Something about the beginning of adventures made us fractious rather than thrilled. It should have felt like a sheet's slow light-filled rise from the line before dropping back down straight again, but instead it started slow like a headache.

*And I need a smoke.*

*We'll get caught.*

*He smokes.*

*Whatever.*

*How much money do you have with you?*

*Back at the house.*

*Jeez, Nylund!*

*Well why'd you leave so fast?*

Daisy had no money because what she got she would spend immediately on whatever had been catching her eye at Woolworth all that week. The smallness of her wants were like the sleek little garden snakes hiding in the leafpiles and sandboxes that might grip against but mostly slide off of your bare arm. Near, real but dissolving. Soon becoming part of everything else.

Now she brought the car to a much protesting halt. There was noone in sight on the gravel road which had deep runoff ditches for shoulders and then the fields rising on both sides of it. First she reversed the car pointlessly and smokily for some twenty yards. Then she turned the car hard to the left and our first wheel made the first stutter over the ditch. I watched the high hard line of the brown field tilt as if from a sudden change of disposition. Then she threw the gear back and wrenched it hard the other way and we were pointed mostly in the right direction though canted off now towards the other shoulder, our back tire testing the descent. She sped us back to our own lane and our own grey house was still sitting there like a grey cake waiting to be remembered.

*Now go in and get it.*

I went into the quiet house and there was nothing to notice. There was a little dish on the bureau and mostly change on it and some half-pulled red tickets from the fair last year. I thought there was some money in the drawer among the socks and I fished around till I felt the paper and I did. I shoved it all in my jeans pocket. I came back out blinking into the sunlight and settled into the car next to Daisy again and we started over.

In the gravel lot outside the Bait N Gas Daisy made me dig it all out of my pocket and hand it crumpled into her hand. I waited in the car. She dallied a pretty long time and then she came out with a plastic bag heavy with provisions, a tabloid sticking out the top. She handed it to me without a word and we drove off again, taking a right and heading nowhere in particular till we just stopped right in the road. We climbed out and over the couple feet of mud and up the quick rising side of the hill. We sat against the fence, my jeans legs getting wet. We could look down at the rusty roof of Big Cousin's car and at the hill beyond it identical to the one we were sitting on, but noone sitting on it. The blue sky rose above it with a blank expression. Daisy smoked and we split the orange soda. We looked at the glossy pictures in the tabloid and Daisy read the stories in a serious voice. There was other stuff in the bag, bubble tape, some trading cards for a game we hadn't heard of, beef jerky. I asked Daisy how she paid for all this stuff and she said they just let her have it, they were nice.

*You stole it.*

*They were nice. They let me have it.*

*You stole it.*

*Nylund, who cares. Who cares about it.*

I opened the packet of trading cards and lifted out the dry, powdery stick of gum. I put it in my mouth, and it tasted awful. I dumped in some orange soda, which helped, but after a few seconds I just spat the whole thing out. There were five cards in the little packet, with cartoon robot drawings on the front. One was a female cartoon robot with a narrow socket waist where the two halves of her machine body met and a little bikini stretched over that. *That's you,* I said, holding it up for her. She looked at it, then brought her thumb and index finger close to it and flicked it away. I held up each of the cards in turn and she flicked them away, over my shoulder and between the white rungs of the fence. They must have settled in the turned earth behind me. Now we were just looking at each other. An earth burial for the robots. Diet of worms. I had a bad taste in my mouth. The vein-hued and the colorless grubs rotoring the soil to get at the cardboard instincts. Wrong stuff in my wiring. Gummed paper guts. Play-brite vinyl sheathing my still copper blood.

# CHAPTER 10
## EAR PIECE, HAIR PIECE, CIGAR BOX

1.

Two white cords drift off to corpus white foam, driftwood worked elaborately along the shoreline. A colossus of stars wadded up on the sky, a colloquy of dazzlers blind to each other's blind. We're blind as the specks on the cheap office ceiling. A duck blind, collapsing. A bridge collapsed in the convoy of shoes. Two hands lock at the thumb; a bird shunts off. A hand gathers out of the crotched sky and probes with an index finger the shallow disk. A bell goes off, a vibration, the vibration of the hammer hitting the roof. *She hit the roof.* The disk spins and prisms. The digital answer jumps to its feet and dives head first out the window. Septimus. Septicemia. *We were so close that when I got an infection in my foot they used the septic pencil on him.* Sarcographic development: telepathic surgery. This body swaddled in neoprene and dunked into the water around the coral reef. This body waiting at the ready in the gleaming hosptical suite that doubles as heaven in the next scene. A caravan of residents winding through, coats made of bedsheets. The narrowness of tropical fish: needlenoze. Razor fin. Their decorated rows of teeth they can drop to the ground like the panties of heiresses in the penthouse suite. The ground is covered with feathers. Played in reverse, they array themselves in showers in the air. Zeus here disguised as golden hair.

2.

Zeus here designed as golden hair. A wax clad easter egg in easter ed. A dividing district. How it is dividing into units and doubling in force. The yolk exerts itself outwards: becomes a gold egg. Parthenogenesis. It fits in the peasant pedestal like a typographical error but keeps being there each time she peers into the room. A tower room a loft room a chest into which one has been chained a veronica of smoke a broidered cape a lanyard of motives and motivations. She motivates like smoke across the flagstone courtyard, over her head a cape. We gathered at the seminary for a family portrait, all the priests carefully sequestered inside. Sidestepping over the groomed hills and long, blandish lanes, trying to find an angle or a vantage point. We walked all the coifed way around. We abandoned the project.

3.

I Dreamed I Saw the Seneca Review in Gold an Indian at the larder or out the lead pane he had a shawl wrapped around him a 500 ct. luxury bedsheet, he traced the lead pane with a finger absently like a woman like he was inside and I out. He appeared without motivation wandering like a fox crossways over the fenced yard and unfenced hills studying the water pump the wheelbarrow the truck's grill which in this scene are rendered in blacks and green with a slick moon slightly parted a sick and memorable fancy.

4.

Cigarillo is right if I could climb that Mt. Madre where the brown hair turns and turn back and allows itself to be secured with pins and bows. Around the crown are ringlets around the temples are wings around the name of the neck unimaginable is a cataract is power is the dam which fires the casinos and dry cleaners and day clinics where the kids slump next to the parents on plastic chairs. They have the waiting room set up like a classroom with rows and rows of old and young and very old and very young and too many middle-aged people for this time of day sitting fivewide and eight deep in the kiddie chairs held up by the straining zippers on their too tight coats. Here is hair: thick mustaches and lovely fat waves that dip back and away; braids; blond hair declaring blackness at the roots; sallow girls whose hair and skin and disdain seem all made of the same materials like gold thinned with milk. A beaten egg. In the rows facing forward. Nothing is before them. Above them, Steve McQueen demonstrates the persecution of the car chase. He leads by example.

# CHAPTER 11
## THE MILLION DOLLAR MOVIE

The Million Dollar Movie comes on at eleven o'clock. We like to watch it slumped down on the green couch with our feet on the floor. With the sound down, it's like flying in a dream carwide over the bay the seals and tourists applauding or through the market the shoppers the barrels hurling upwards their tomatoes and eggs or in through the sunbay of the museum we anchor the rope to the copter's leg our dart guns snug in our jeans. We grab it all and run. We are devotees of The Movie, slumped in its dovecoat. Out in the henyard, we practice kung fu slo mo and then scatter the grain in slow spirals. We duck under each other's fankicks and we eat it all up. Then we throw up and collapse in the henyard, breathing through our down coats until the world goes rightside up.

If you breathe too close to the land you get the bird flu, we know that now. Then, no. If you breathe too high up in the air the air thins out and you see as through a fog of particulates blindly and if you look at things through a mirror on your birthday then the scales fall from your eyes. Then your eyes are ready for cooking, miss junior bride. Miss junior lucy. God help me I'm a leper and the scales have fall from my eyes. *I made you this way on purpose so you'd be a better beggar.*

Says god.

I made you look like the king so you could switch with him and play out the Benevolent Despot. I'm playing the Benevolent Despot today and I'll share my juicy fruit with you. And my cell and my flagolet and a ride around the fountain in my nimble ship the Effete Kipper. It was a present to me from the fish and if you look in its tiny portholes you see a tiny gallery with the paintings of all the other kids they blessed this way staring out dolefully from under black crimped wigs in gold frame-ups.

It's like shooting gallery. The ducks go by on tracks. The weather ducks eastward for Georgia and the other side of the tracks. Out of eyeline, it whips off its potato sack disguise and muscles on the fleecy cravat of the high quality cloud structure.

Shoots an arrow back through the air: adorned with the king's penchant. By the order of the king. C'mover here, cutie.

By the order of the king we assemble at the discotheque. Here are an endless supply of girls, mostly with tooth problems that keep them out of the film circles. They wear placards decked with road signs—triangular, chevronic—they feature an arrow rampant or crooked or tied around itself with a sly over the shoulder glance at the passerby. These legends are by the same favorite who painted the king's portrait at (the king's) age of four when he was prince-sized; the portraitist is not himself in the scene but can be seen in the easel the way it cants under its burden. The sightlines in his work reflect his malnutrited bones or broken arches or bloodbones stamped by hooves. That's the mark of luck. The cramped spine of waterjug this wench is dressed as, that checkerbox flexing like it holds the covenant itself. When the water drops in note by note through the leaky ceiling, then a chord charades, and then mote by mote a chainmail assembles which, thrown in the spot, coats gold, and it's the grand finale. Cymbals bite the air. The girls all gyrate like the end of the world.

One Halloween *Know what I am?* asks Daisy, her hair pulled back from each temple, her pulled eyes gritty with blue glimmery eyeshadow, her lips hot pink, light pink strokes up each cheek bone. She wears a grey sweater tight over a white tee shirt and a silver short skirt and black tights with holes and sneakers. She looks like herself. But she's The Million Dollar Movie.

# CHAPTER 12
## TIME IS BRAIN

Rose's grandson arrived at the apartment with his brain leaping out of his skull. Long silver lashes and burbling white effusions rose and made an atmosphere around his flattish luminant head. His pale skin was waxy and looked carved by the sunken heat of his eyes. Looking at him was like looking sharply northward into the wind, or with an error in your eye. His image bled and streamed around you.

In a long military overcoat, he tilted into the room. Deep white carpets, lion-footed chests, sleek drapery elegant as a woman's gown and her pale arms, her wrists tucked behind her. Rose the glare that fell on lamps and glasstops, the finish on her acetylene robe. Nylund the acrid filigree of ash sinking into the fabrics, the unreadable smoke rings in the ceiling. Grandson the quicksilver torch shone roughly into the corners and cabinets, over the mantels.

Nylund had the fantasy of mold growing in the collecting pools of light. A second coming. A species assembling shields and plaques, a settling of placards over the upright struts of temples, the erecting of a plinth from which florid platitudes would be scattered, a vinyl-tinged vomiting up of flame. The flame would cook the clouds, the clouds would melt down the open mouth of a thin shunt of fused beach sand, and in this vein would grow the Grandson, plus a storm-stained garden of thorned fistshapes where Rose repeated herself like a figure in a carpet, again and again.

This Rose brought in little glasses hemmed in by gold on a thin gold tray that nearly disappeared as she held it at eye level. Liquor for him and for herself and for the Grandson who was constantly in motion. Like a bored actor, he lifted his hand in a flat interrogative gesture or tapped his temple or drove his fist into his hip in swinging time with his tempo.

"Long days, grandmother. We have been too long separated."

"Inattention on my part, but you know I am a bachelor."

"I awake in the morning to see the broad mirror on my bureau, reflecting on the white plaster wall above my head."

"They study each other constantly, except when I come between them."

"I feel like a jealous child."

"Do they know that I'm watching, just feet below, as they gorge on each other?"

"I have taken a job at a bank."

"It is entirely made of marble like a gentleman's souvenir."

"Coming to it is like taking my place in a cabinet."

"Like a droll doll in a curio. It is a pleasurable feeling."

"Our actions in the bank are small."

"We hold them at arm's length."

"It seems we are always seated, but, then, we must cross short distances marked out in squares in the polished floor."

"It seems a struggle to make progress because of the depth of polish."

"I have friends there, and other friends who would like a job there."

"I can't vouch for everyone. Vernaculars of smoke."

"On the top level are the big bosses."

"I'd like to smoke out their windows and watch the people passing below and rest my hand on the stone eagles."

"Vernaculars."

"You are always watched at the bank. The girls wear their hair combed like money, over their eyes."

"But the clocks have beautiful blank faces, like someone retrieving a memory in sleep."

"It's loud here, even when it's quiet. How do you sleep?"

"The water keeps dripping off the eaves onto the doorstep. It'll wear a saddle in it."

"Over a long, long time."

"Right, Nylund?"

"Some rich fool walks by with a bunch of yappy dogs."

"Like motors at shin level."

"You're going the same way but at a slower pace."

"Maybe slowed down by the girl tucked under your arm. That's alright."

"Your shouldered edifice, your hat like a roof."

"When will you both arrive?"

"Him first, in the marble waiting room, running a bored finger over the glossed breasts of the magazine rack."

"Considering drinking some coffee for the distraction."

"I'd like to smoke at the bank among the big stone angels."

"And the one in the nightgown with the scales and her eyes closed."

"Like she's afraid to see what's happening."

"Or wants to say she didn't know."

"But she's the one with the sword in her hand!"

"There's all sorts of machines to tell the future now."

"Poured in cast iron or brought in from Japan."

"Tell you and your girl what your kids will look like."

"I like to think of all those futures out there, nailed in a row."

"Like plastic ducks, a token a shot."

The Grandson delivered his lines steadily, a needle on an arm in his gut. Rose kept up a countertide of little birdy gestures. She wore a purple folded turban over her head. She settled disks on the phonograph, klinked and refilled glasses, sat and stood. She swept out of the room and in.

Abruptly, the Grandson sat down on the couch and stopped talking. The silence was acute and metallic, as if Nylund and Rose must now pour language into the bowl. Then it changed colors, rose up from the floor like sound off a cymbal, touched each of their faces and their ears. This was a warming feeling, a flush that felt scarcely external. Nylund sank back. The Grandson leaned forward. Rose's position was somewhere in between, which is to say, upright. A new shoot.

"Well," she said drily, as if uttering words that had been drafted her by some hack. "And what will you do now?"

"Just now, Grandmother, I've got to go." He got to his feet.

"*Just* now? As in this instant?" Rose was uncharacteristically shrill, and her mouth was distended, as if she were physically expelling the words from her mouth.

"Yes, Grandmother. I've got to meet a friend and pick up some belongings. I've already asked Nylund to come." He looked at Nylund and Nylund felt a pointed candle meditatively licking him over. He nodded.

"I don't quite believe it," Rose said. "But goodbye, gentlemen. Noone is keeping you here against your will."

The Grandson leaned down, kissed his grandmother, and reached a hand behind him, collaring Nylund. With this man suspended at arm's length from his wrist like either a prized or dubious fish, he charged out of the apartment, in and then out of the nimbus of light thrust by his own uncanny hair.

# CHAPTER 13
## DRAG

The gust furled all up around them an like an intricate dress of cold. It folded; frilled; uncurled; carried them into arcades of dark and boxy wind. They felt hands reach down from the limbs of trees, grab their wrists, and swing them forward, and they felt little licking twig-needles reach up for their ankles and feel along their shins. Nothing besides this motion impelled them deeper. After a while he was able to peer out of their glamor, and he felt as if he should be far above the scene, looking down on the landscape from wide sloping wings, the houses like gel-caps scattered over the hills. From this height he would like to spit out his teeth. He thought of the flimsy latches that held bathroom doors closed. Flimsy matches that could burn up a household a million times. Switch train to a new track.

The chassis was packed with movie magazines, the only thing in the Cousins' house that had once been of any value, except for their uniforms which they had to buy from the plant itself but weren't worth stealing. The magazines had the worn lustre of money. They chronicled decades. The same stars would emerge as arm's-length girls or scraps of boys, would mature and bloom, and pose and fade and bend down again small as they had begun, under the arbitrary Clotho of the photo editor. These stars would start out hard and silver like the inside of a soup-can phone to whisper to the other side of the room where your sister, through her dirty brown hair, was listening through the cold forest of her pulse. A hand found a switch a switch was thrown and they burst into color, life-like, hibiscoid and non-animal pinks yellows greens past health would wilt completely in this overblown ease.

Now folded into worn stapled covers and stacked up in the back: like maps.

In wells below the front seat, candy corn and necklaces, Cokes, a schoolbook on conquistadors, feet of Nylund and Daisy, heavy socks and thin sneakers. Daisy steered the long square nose of the car over the width of the country and through the cold piercable fabric of the night. Eventually she just stopped the car in the middle of the road. The moonlight held the car in place. He watched the white exhaust pile up like slung bolts in the rear view and where he laid the side of his fist against the window a white star bloomed up. The fields rose steeply and briefly around them like lines of blue black laundry.

"Keep on or go back, Nylund."

It was a question but with her newly orange hair splatting the thick collar of her brown nylon jacket and her real cold red lips she said it flatly like an ultimatum. Nylund nodded: descent, ascent. Milk and candy had been their diet for days, and their skin was dusted over with some kind of lunar precipitate, kiss of milk on the last day, dusting for fingerprints in advance. Before you're corpseworn. Diet of worms. Sell by the last day, and/or he'll raise you up. The vice squad pouring the milk down gutters, circa the Milk Wars, unpasteurized wheals in the dust. Well overland the big dairy where the atomic knuckle had rose up a redundancy in the afternoon sky. They had no choice but to take it in, gather it up, pulp it for neatness' sake: no waste. Then shine with ex-eyes, cry with roses for lungs. The milk that shattered bottles. The blood that breaks down walls. Scratch that: the love. Love cabal, hit parade. The hits raining down all night from the satellite. From troopship to tract home, the scrubbed hand that launches the sub to the gloved hand that pulls the lever and lowers milkshake down into waxy takeout cups: love.

Nylund et Daisy, driving for the milkbar of the city, stained with sodium, neon, copper, lead dust, that leaks the box and causes ink to spoil. The city necropolish, bakelite, wiped slick and buzzing bright with flies. The green eyes of the convenience store spook, his nursey smock. The tines and the coin. The tissue paper cross hatch of the moon. Lay it against your top lip: hum. Trace it on the mealy paper. What else could be fit between the drawn thumb and the finger, rubber band, the signature of grease. In-love of the brother and sister. Thereafter she had the nervousest fingers. Ankles emerging from the purple jeans. The splayjawed zippers, wrists. They wanted a box to get inside, but they kept splitting. So they ended. Some months. The instances multiply. Nylund lands feet first at the soup kitchen. Daisy-mine, sprained, badly healed is soonest mended, won't stay.

Wicks off into the night. Gold purse on a chain. Glints one last time like a gas to flame.

# CHAPTER 14

Nylund tuned way up beyond what his senses can bear. His face a bloodhound's: flanged, and flared. He has to keep pushing forward to keep this busy flesh furled out. He's a working breed. The Grandson walks a beat before, and as he passes under the brainpan of each streetlamp his silver hair lights like a fuse or like a pyramid of powder like a roomful of gas going up. They work down the long street: whump, whump, whump.

Nylund's hat angled over one eye like a knife blade orbital. Like a one-eyed oracle he sees partially with his open eyes but forsooth with his eyes wholly closed: wholly. He knows in acrid smoke. He knows in a scent going up. They were moving towards the house of bad business. On closed eyes, one mercurial clot was drawing itself thin in the direction of this outcome.

Nylund at last: perfected sarcography. Sees the eidolon numbers coming into view on his closed lids: six—or nine. Dyslexic mind. Three or e. Seven minutes at the Seven-Eleven.

Heaven,
snake eyes.
A nose for knowing,
A nose like two gravecars, gardener, two grottoes for double sons, multiply by every snake in the sea, tulipy, lily death, to fit your snout inside, like a u-cone: double-wide.

Breath.

They are inside like a puff of smoke snaking the keyhole. Hello. The tiled hallway's a cold, sacred feeling. A box in praise of light. Too soft, yellow-hued through the transom. You couldn't live on it. The glass is braced with optimistic diamonds. To keep the sound inside.

Blow through the next like a fuse blowing out. A ripple in the Grandson's meticulous fingers.

In the parlor like a taper on the Thames. The theme is: river rats. Red eyes shrinking but the inner dish widening for light.

Light thrown from the Grandson's thin skull; leaves a trail of light as he ducks to left and right. He knows what he's looking for, hands under the flat of the cushions. Nylund studies the enamel screen propped in front of the fireplace. It catches light in weird ways. Two nymphs reach out of swoony cattails and point at each other; cock their fingers in the shape of guns. Squint their eyes. The guns are dragonflysized. At the base of the firescreen, a rock-shaped hump— is it a rabbit leaping forward? No. It is the toe of a man's shoe standing behind Nylund. He wheels around: the Grandson, eyes darting around the huge lakey mirror over the mantel. Then he ducks away again and into another room. The room goes dark. Streetlight leans calmly through the windowdrape, bending slightly at its belted waist. Nylund hears clatter from the kitchen, the whine of the Grandson opening up the oven door, the thud of him getting down on his knees to pat behind it. Little profane sparking rivulets.

"There's nothing *in here*, Nuh-Nuh-Nylund!" he hisses

as if it had been Nylund's idea to come here. Nylund hears this hissing multiplied, a-chorale. Then, revising his pessimism, the Grandson charges back into the sitting room: "Help me with this." The two men of mismatched heights struggle to lift the heavy mirror off the wall and lean it against the sofa. The Grandson runs his hands over the back, leaving black streaks of soot. He swears and raises his two hands like a surgeon. He runs his hands through his hair. The room goes dark. Instinct fails them. It is impossible to know if the intricately and expressively creased dark is actually arcs of soot, fingerprint laden, chiaroscuroed with the Grandson's here-I-am. The Grandson stumbles back into the kitchen and fumbles for the faucet. He leaves it running. He runs back in.

"Shit, Nylund did you touch anything?"

"I don't have a r-record."

"But if they see anything's been touched they'll dust the whole place!"

"Should we turn the lights on?"

"That's a big risk. Someone will definitely see the lights go on in here."

"Just for a second. We can see what's what."

Nylund's hand meets the switch midair like asking a lady to dance. He pauses. The girls in the screen giggle like underwater; or is it the slim reeds; or some people down in the foyer; or is it some part of him. He switches the light on:

The light on: the room full: a bowl of marigoldglass dunked in water and about to break with its weight. The carpet's wrecked pink. The wallpaper flowers have withdrawn, modestly, and pulled the dust over them. The room bare except for the green couch tufted and vegetal. But no obvious fresh prints in the carpet. No prints on the switch or the wall. Dust undisturbed on the mantel. The Grandson runs bent into the kitchen. Runs out, his coat sleeve dark where he's dried off the sink. They grasp the thick mirror by its sunrays and lift it back up to the wall. Nylund snaps the light out.

They are blind; then the room sinks down around them.

Their faces now rise in the mirror, pale and precise like the faces of the drowned in dreams: like the young ghosts of the place.

# CHAPTER 15

This lemon yellow bilious sweet. This eyes-closed creamy blissing through it. Is it a taste or a touch. Spread like a sheet like a custard curtain across the rise of his cheeks. His closed eyes. What a temple. His temples. It's cool, it's got a sharp edge. It's cool, it lays against his cheek, his throat. He feels it tickle at the corner of his eye.

A ringing. An old phone. A girl with identifiable hair, carrot braids upon braids, sheets of still dishwater, night-gowns, smocks, overalls, straps, moves all these garments, reaches through the cool husk of light, through the hup hup of, the sound a fan makes, the other kind of lightness, a lack of bodily weight, though the whole scene is heavy. Fingers on his shoulders. Yanked to a window frame he's delighted she's as rough as a child. Now she spreads out and is a fog over the entire city, a city of the movies, he sees it through his eyes closed, reels and sprockets and film-black holes he feels the view folding around his head, cooling his ear and his aching neck. Something locks around his ankles, the blood fills his head like a slow idea. A slow conclusion he cannot quite reach. His hands joined behind him simple as a boy's. Is he humble or does he have a secret in them. Does he have a humble secret in them. A ringing. The city shifts. Shirtbox sky scrapers settling down to a goldgreen bay on a regular, deterministic slope. A hand without a ruler drew these lines. Yellow pipe cleaners unraveled form the rivulets of light. High on the slope, lobes of glue join rickety balconies to the tenements. Where the glass should be, neat squares of aluminum foil rippled with glue. Wherever he looks he can see closer and closer but more fake.

He is thinking 'no people' when he feels himself set against a huge concrete shoulder, face forwards, helpless as a baby, and his eyes closing very close up to the hand-colored sky.

*

Nylund is hauled in from the window and tossed against the white floor. He's thrown by his shoulders into a closet and the door is closed. The closet is empty. The closet is not empty. Above him, wire hangers tilt pacifically on the bar. He sees their thin motion before he feels it high above his head. Therefore the closet is not completely dark. A white line of light at its base. Two green smoking eyes directly across from him. A fringe of silver glowing hair. The Grandson. The Grandson is staring at him. No. The Grandson is staring at his chest. At the middle of his chest where sentimentalists would have his heart, but Nylund knows it is to the left of that, corresponding to his sense of a life off-balance. Nylund himself looks down. A soft nimbus rises through his thin white shirt, and, closing his eyes, Nylund can feel the shape of the object casting the light, a weight so light as to barely register. Teeth in his chest.

# CHAPTER 16
## OF COURSE

Of course it is a key. Of course it is a comb. Of course it is a haystack. It is a mouth full of needles. One needle clasps another. One hand reaches for a hand: it hurts (joy buzzer) or it shares a shock. A shock like a million needles. Volt: the batsign. The real batsign is shit. The searchlights comb the low sky over the perimeter or the premiere. And can comb it again and again when there is no premier. Marking every perimeter. An endlessly inlooping perimeter like a fingerprint or a mountain on a contour map. Nylund has his textbook in his lap. Cockroaches think at their periphery but they don't breathe there. The big sedan like a boat reaches the city then is too leaky to continue. It dies at a gas station. They are sitting outside it. They have no money for gas. The cashier takes the money through a low amber Plexiglas window. It is four o'clock in the morning. Men shamble up to the window or step up to the window, men with curlers in their hair, women with the situation draped all over them and sending out a steer-clear in every direction. A bug trapped in amber could be thousands of years old, a road paved with porphyry meaning purple, the biology of building materials, digested by cockroaches roaming geography. They take the pulse points with them. They move at the infrastructure of the house, could that be its periphery. Central in one sense, integral, literally marginal. Like people moving through the city. Quiet by five A.M. Waiting for something to happen to them.

At five the white truck breaks the break in the traffic and pulls up to park. The new clerk unlocks the door. It's morning and not night, the sky coming grey. The huge white metal tumblers in the bed are searchlights. Daisy and Nylund get off their feet, their legs feel skinny and stiff. They walk into the grey-lit convenience store and cruise the four stubby aisles of sunflower seeds and air-freshener. The truck driver is paying for coffee and microwaving some kind of plastic-wrapped sandwich. They follow him out to his truck.

"Can you turn on your lights for us, Mister." Daisy asks. Her eyes are like doorknobs. Dishtowels. Dishes. Her eyes are a whole house.

"Can you ask me nicer."

"Please."

"Can you come up in the truck and ask me nicer."

"No."

Nylund feels like a drainpipe.

"Shit," the man says, with some relief. He hands the bag and cup to Daisy and climbs into his cab. "Look out for each other," he says and drives off.

Next time it is Daisy who drives off. "Wait here for a half hour," she says to Nylund over her shoulder, climbing into the car. After two hours he wonders if he could walk into the city; he can see the guardrail over the freeway that marks the limit. After two more hours he's hungry. He drinks the lukewarm coffee that tastes like paper which makes his stomach go square. Coffee that's lost its warmth is room temperature but he's not in a room. He's outside a convenience store, it's one of the longest days he can remember, nine in the morning, disgusting and tempting smells from the microwave mnemonic of digestion, another of his textbook's glossy and well labeled and useless maps.

*

He opens his mouth and shuts it: pop-pop. The Grandson's eyes are closed, his hair smoking. In the room, people are dragging chairs; one clatters down and is cursed back to its feet. Then the closet door is yanked open, Nylund and the Grandson dragged by the collars into the middle of the roomful of afternoon light. The windows are opaque with light; they are up in the air. Then on their backs like Samsa, their free legs bent like feelers. The Grandson has composed himself and is glaring up into the hatbrims of the three faceless men. Nylund's cockroach body works on the coordinates of the room. It is a large rectangular room, painted white. Vinyl floor. Doors at either end and a door to the hall; a wall of windows. Nylund senses he has been in this room before, in this almost identical box of light, tinted a shade darker. He is way up high in the house of bad business. He is in one of the apartments signified by the invisible numbers missing inside the lobby door, but also on a city street. There is not much more these three men can do to them without risking attention. Also, they have not been industrious enough to haul him and the Grandson out by night. This suggests that they do not know quite what they are doing or after. Rather than calming Nylund, this makes his heart thump in his chest. They are under orders from someone. Everything is happening at a remove: being acted out here in the numberless apartment on the nameless floor. Being directed somewhere else.

Two men stand at Nylund's and the Grandson's heads, their hands in the pockets of their grey overcoats. In the daylit room, they are dressed in shadows. The third sits in a chair at their feet. Everyone stares at each other as if they don't know how to begin.

"Now, boys," begins the seated man. "The item you took from that young lady's apartment, we'll have to have it back. Everyone likes a memento, a pentimento, a memory-by. A lovely girl, we're like a fanclub. Skin like a handrail, like an up staircase, like the golden thread that holds the service car to the pulley and tugs: That kind of girl. A girl/gone by. It makes us/sentimental. We'd like a/memento. We couldn't possibly enter the crimescene, the crimessence, and take one as you scamps have. And yet we find ourselves with the/upperhand in this situation. We believe we'll take yours."

"We voted," one of the other toughs adds.

"Yeah we voted. As a club. So hand it over."

"Wuh-we didn't f-find anything in the apartment," Nylund says. Through the floor, he senses a stirring through the building, and this reassures him. The Grandson can't say anything through his gag. The man in the chair nods, and something heavy swings down into Nylund's line of sight. He braces for the impact but it's the Grandson who's clipped on the side of the head. He makes a high-pitched, infuriated noise, his acid glare bucketing out, reviving to pour down his cheeks and surge towards the interrogator, who now turns his own attention on Nylund.

"Look, young person. Unlike your freak friend here who

chooses his disturbance, you seem disadvantaged by nature. I feel sympathy for you, I feel a natural sense of balance regarding your person, in short, I don't feel like doing further injury to your brain. I'm not sure how this silver-haired incorrigible talked you into infiltrating this building but you're here now, regardless, and I want back whatever it is you took from that apartment. Now!"

The afternoon is waning. Through his back and hands pressed together, Nylund feels children coming home, women returning with shopping, radios searching for frequency, partylines ringing, gas hissing through valves. He knows these valves, these values, these walls and signals, knows just how to elapse through them, but is uncertain, now, as to his obligations to the Grandson, whether to leave the Grandson behind.

He opens his mouth. Pop. Fishy. He lets his gaze roll up to the white ceiling, its white-on-white mottles and pits.

"What is he, having a fit?" tough #2 asks.

"No." Nylund says, breathing evenly, studying the lunar bays. *It is the dark mares we are seeing when we speak of the Man in the Moon. When we speak of. What we are see-ing.* Tranquility and fecundity. The sea that has become known to us, seas of crisis and cleverness. The sea of moisture, the sea of showers, nectar, cold. A sea of edges. That was the sea Nylund is looking upon.

"Wuh-we are at an impasse," Nylund says, and is clocked in the head and shoved bodily back in the closet.

\*

Her summer homework is to make a pinhole camera and his summer homework is make a timecapusle. She's looked all over for the right kind of container and can only find big, damp cardboard boxes rotting around magazines or emptied of food. Nothing small enough to hold in the hands that also keeps out light. Her project is temporarily suspended. He also needs a box and is using a sock for now, shoving everything inside. The time capsule is supposed to be a record of himself and his family. He shoves inside a cigarette, a matchbox car, a plastic magnifying lens the size of his thumb, one plastic daisy hairclip, the cover off a movie magazine. That's it. He slinks it on the table. Then he fishes for the magnifying lens and looks at the weave of the sock; it's not much more than you can see with the naked eye, just bigger. There's a hole, at any rate, at the heel and you can see the paper and plastic sticking out from inside. The sock is dirty and smooth around the hole. When he holds the sock by the throat, the hole gets bigger. He clunks it on the offwhite linoleum table. Sunlight is washing through the nylon curtains over the window which is dark grey at the top with bugs on the other side. When he looks right into it with his eyes closed little prints develop on his lids, bright blood-orange on blood. He can't look long enough to figure out what the prints are of. He opens his eyes and the room is blacked out. Daisy is up on a chair reaching for a can of salt. That might do for the camera, but will have to be cut up. She opens the spout of the can and begins pouring the salt out into a saucepan sitting on the stove. It forms a bright white sash from her hand to the black pan. The yellow and purple girl on the can is a smudgy flower next to Daisy's hand folded around it, her green fingernails. Daisy wants to smoke the cigarette from his time capsule. He whines about it, but what can he do. She reaches in through the hole in the sock and yanks it out. It's crooked. The sock is totally ruined now. She lights the cigarette off the kitchen stove, pushing the salt out of the way. She sits and smokes, then she takes the lit end to the edge of the salt canister to burn a pinhole through. The cardboard catches fire and both children squeal as she tosses it into the sink and runs the water onto it. It's smoldering. "Wow, wow!" is all they can say, and then they want to be outside and far away from it. They run through the high grass of the yard and to the treeline and then into the trees, where they slow down and look back towards the house for flame or smoke in the sky. They press deeper to wet mulchy ground and a tree trunk to sit against. They sit on the soaking, inflammable ground and think about the house, stacked with paper, lined with paper inside. Is it there now, will it be gone when they get back.

# CHAPTER 17

Sunk to the bottom of the closet. The light cast green-ish from the Grandson's shuteyed and sunken face. The key or the comb settled against Nylund's sternum. His ribs, a little current like an eddy or static snagging the settled field. The future assembled like hairpins turned to bullets by the MRI machinery like moths to a flame like humans to a set-up: it can only go one way. It begins like a piece of slapstick. Coin-sized moths assemble on the sheet fastened to the rungs of two ladderback chairs sunk into the garden. Moth the size of a hand open for a slap or a cut flaps greenly on the porch floor. Peeling thick blue paint still looks liquid. It is losing some kind of dust that lets them fly and read the night light. Patches of paint leaping off the porch swing as if it were on fire. It is a kind of fire, oxygen changing the chains. A regular bulb from a houselamp has been screwed into the socket above the porch. It burns too brightly and through a flag or an army of bugs in the air. The air thick as lake water. It can burn up all this night.

Two legs and then four legs leave the apartment. That leaves two legs left. They are waiting. The light a little blue in the crack under the door. The room begins to breathe, not ethereally, as one might expect of a twilit room, but thickly, a long heavy breath thrust roughly out as if pushed by a broom. The last guard is sleeping.

The Grandson's eyes open quick as a cat's, the pupil splits vertically and casts a lime-colored glow. Nylund now sees that he's always crushing something to produce that glow. He's always using something up. Nylund looks for something in himself to crush. Fireflies in the hand, the milk-yellow glow and the nervey red skin. Sugar candy like bottle glass under the sneaker sole. Thin sheets of carbon paper. Green grids and lines. Lines of force. Crush it all down.

He feels that green keenness come into his own eyes. He can see behind his back. He turns a beam on his bound wrists, and he works the tight knot free. His aching hands lift automatically and make a horizontal sweep—a thick green grass seems to rise in the dark between them. A smoky rain odor. They rise thigh deep in it. He unfastens the Grandson's hands and pulls the gag away. Briefly the Grandson's eyes roll back like money but return to place. They steady themselves in the suave, milky light that is falling from inside of them. The ceiling of the closet rises high as night. Nylund grabs a few inches of the Grandson's sleeve to anchor him. Then he touches his palm to the closet door and pushes it lightly open.

The darkness of the room is lighter than the darkness of the closet, softer. They glide into it almost too liquidly. The thug isn't much of a thug, sleeping with his ankles crossed, chair tilted back against the wall opposite. His flatgrey trenchcoat hangs away from him classically, riplettes of light, the silvery scarf at his throat, a black immateriality where his face should be. Above this floats the perfect illustration of a fedora. It seems almost to be drawn on the air: felt that expands to touch the moonlight or streetlight; the generous, hand-plotted curve of the brim and carefully dented crown like the ear that sleeps in itself. What the palm knows. Story it wants to get back to telling itself. Nerve network. Ear deep at sleep on the floor of the porch.

\*

"Clocks, Nyluuund!" It was a not-too rare moment of idleness on the floor and the Superior was demonstrating to Nylund the finer points of haberdashery his own person embodied. At this moment he had his trouser leg raised to reveal a blue-grey sock with a white and gold seal woven just above the ankle. A black strap was clipped to the sock and ran out to garter at the man's thin, shiny white shin. With a wag of his heel the Superior let his thin blue-grey pantleg fall back into place. He settled on his feet, dragged his legs together, clicked his gleaming heels, and, like a Marine, took a half step forward before wheeling to turn to Nylund his back. He stuck an index finger in either side of his jacket to pull it taut. "Vents!" He swung back around, heels clicking, and stopped with his two hands pointing at the floor to show the straight lines of his jacket and a hint of cuff covering the tops of his hands. "Cuffs," he barked, grinning, enjoying his display too much to maintain the proper rigor. Then, bending his elbows like Carmen Miranda, he crowed, "Links!"

Leaning in close to Nylund, who was himself resting against a thickly polished endtable, he shoved his throat up into Nylund's line of sight. Minute gold and purple diamonds paved its swellings and withdrawals. "Knot! Study it! It is too difficult for you, but I am here as an example, even for unattainable goals." As he said this, he opened his hands, raised his eyes to the chandeliers, the attitude of the drill sergeant now totally lost. He sank into the nearest elaborately upholstered gold wing chair and raised his closed eyes heavenward. "Ah, Nylund!" he said. "I have the passion, the discipline, but not the raw desire to be a true leader in this field." He opened one eye and looked at Nylund. "I think you'll find that nothing about me is raw at all. Except, Nylund, my nerves on days as frantic as this." The hiss of his final letter charged the entire showroom. The gloss on the floor insisted it was its own element, not a surface of something else. The huge dark wooden tables reached down to clutch polished orbs as if holding worlds in place. Nylund wasn't sure what model of the universe would look like this, the planets like so many outsized marbles trapped in the claws of the gods, life itself clotted and materialized as leaping deer and floral showers worked in gold thread to heavy fabrics that, hung from the ceiling, dampened all the noise from the surrounding floors. The ceiling itself was recognizable; hung with chandelier after chandelier it was the original crystal sphere, one dislodged sector of the formerly unimaginable firmament of heaven.

When Nylund first came to work here he felt ambivalent about the hyper-decorativeness of the showrooms. Home Furnishings was deserted almost all the time, kept running by a kind of nostalgia on the part of the superannuated bachelor heir who was the head head of the corporation's board of heads. Yet except for the afternoons of boardmeetings when these heads would gather at some unimaginably altitudinous secret compartment of the buildings, he, the medium sized pastry-white heir, did not spend any time at the store, let alone in this, the Superior's formal court. There were side and antechambers here, a rather pleasant acreage of porcelain sinks and gleaming mirrors fitted with showgirl bulbs, erotically empty bathtubs lit from above and lifting an inviting oval nimbus towards those who stood too close by to see their delicate, pawlike feet, and a decidedly déclassé wing of rec and rumpus rooms which invited a disproportionate share of foottraffic. The kitchen showroom struck Nylund as the most eerie, like a scrupulously dusted wax museum, the laminate dining sets and gridded, grated appliances destined never to be used.

His favorite task in the showroom was to apply extra cleanser and polish to the surfaces which the Superior declared had not yet attained a baroque enough level of gleam. Nestled in the polish fumes and feeling the flexible chamois glide over the turned and beveled legs and arm rests, joints and feet, Nylund felt his mind itself stretch and bend in sarcography. An entirely unhumanoid consciousness, without even the shape of mind, running, dribbling, flooding, bounding, bouncing, collecting and pooling across a series of cool and curving planes. This space was dark. He seemed always about to enter a nimbus, but did not. It had time, then, a constantly suspended moment. Reflecting on this period of material, mindless consciousness, Nylund wondered if he had been conscienceless, too. Yes, if without culture. No, if conscience is a continual weighing, a system of substances in space, an inclination towards a non-inclination. A full, or an emptied balance.

# CHAPTER 18

Their bodies are sore, the night less familiar to them for the incredible lengths they've gone to to free themselves into it. As they walk down the street of shadows, Nylund's wrist tenders every kink and current in the night air that hits against it. The Grandson moves rapidly in front of him with his chin up, as is his habit, hurrying in long strides down the sidewalks and across the intersections to carry himself as rapidly as possible away from the scene of the adventure, without considering that he is only hurrying their arrival at the next. When Nylund occasionally gets abreast of him, he can see the Grandson's distended jaw shift greenly, but whether the Grandson is carrying on some conversation with himself or testing his sore apparatus Nylund can't say.

He himself is allowing his mind to think of anything but their predicament. He's lost in networks, the slender pipe-and-bloom sprinkler heads that grid office ceilings, lacy copper inside walls, this city, seen from above, and himself in it, moving around the grid like... information, he guesses, but right now he feels not a lot like that. He doesn't know, has never known anything, and yet images keep presenting themselves to be read, fists, bouquets of animated bees that spread out to perform a half-time show, gyrations which amount to 'fields of sweet grass and clover, over there,' and over there, passing through that knowledge communicated, grassy hillocks like the shoulders of giants turn to him, and now she's epithetic, turns to him her flowery face and smiling breast, and he clambers to the top and is lost in his sense of dry grass and sun, the stirring of little insects, bee sounds in the shell of his ear. He's dazzled as a child, his trenchcoat drying in the sun and lifting to ripple in the wind like a strange and imageless flag.

Pupa. Wings of colorless skin, pale shroud to be borne through. Call me Caul. I was born blind, means I have only my first sight, what you'd call your second. Blinded with everything extra. Nylund rises up. He rises with unsinking footsteps and wafts over the hill. Landscape comes to him like curtains to push through, curtains of pine, fog, hazy air over meadows. He comes to the edge of their small lot, moves forward without feeling the grass to his knees. He stops at the kitchen window, sees the house as they've lived in it, but abandoned, a starburst of coffee on the wall, shards of red cup stuck to it and raying out across the floor, an open package of saltines strewn lovingly on the laminate table, movie magazines piled against the walls where girls in their once-neat bonnets drown in profile beneath grease and dirt, refuse to admit it and move. *Admit it. Admit it.* A yellowish green fixedness fills the room like a solid presence. He is standing with both his hands to his cheeks. Is he crying? Is he dead?

"We're not dead," he says to the Grandson as they balance like swimmers in the light beneath a streetlamp. Should they be hiding? They each take a step back until their chests and legs are in light but their faces hidden in a supple curving bank of blackness.

"They'll be looking for us," the Grandson replies evenly.

"Maybe. They weren't such good thugs."

"Nylund, we're… distinctive," he says, running his hand through his head of fuses.

"You're distinctive. I look like nobody."

"Except for that glowing thing around your neck."

"Yes."

"What is it?"

"I haven't looked at it."

"Should we have a look at it?"

"Should we cut your hair?"

"I'd consider it."

But later, back in Nylund's apartment, he screams when they do it, pink water streaming from his scalp, and the towel comes away spotted red like an unreal hide. He folds up his shorn hair in a piece of newspaper, and then he leaves, dull-eyed like a limping animal, his face so crushed as to be featureless.

The key hangs at Nylund's neck like a bone in his throat. Standing in the cubicle bathroom, feeling the metallic grit of the Grandson's hair beneath his feet, he undoes the first few buttons of his shirt and holds it open. The key is not, in fact, glowing. It is light brown, a housekey, average. It is heavy to look at but its heaviness disappears again as Nylund pushes the buttons of his shirt through their waiting holes. Then he walks automatically to his narrow cot and collapses into sleep.

# CHAPTER 19

Sunlight and light ringing all around him—Nylund at the center of a thousand coin-colored rings bouncing against each other for joy in the light. He sat up abruptly, his alarmclock went dead on its own. Had it been ringing like this every morning since his absence? Had he been absent? He placed a hand to his chest. The key which had magically appeared there had not magically disappeared. Nylund was not quite use to it but felt a kind of proprietorship over it like a new scar. He felt himself smiling dumbly. Was it now time to stand up from his bed, make breakfast, all the dumb and birdy rituals of a private morning? It was, he thought, standing up, looking with fondness at his bland plastic cups and plates on their shelf wearing their fading pajama-colored stripes. Opening his refrigerator vault a terrible current swept over him and he slammed it shut. So he had been gone from this place at least a little while. Bad milk.

He hunched over a meal which entered his system like it had always been part of it— animal products forming solids and liquids, clinging to plates, toast, tissues, each other, being swallowed, washed away, boiled, reformed. He liked hunching here amid the other backs and elbows and lowered heads and sweaty faces—unexeceptional again. The waitress held aloft her aluminum coffeepot like Molly Pitcher, her auburn hair curled lightly over her shoulder, her eyes shining with all the lights of thirteen stars. Nylund was happy. If from the corner of his eye he thought he beheld one of last night's thugs, positioning his visage-abyss above a plate of homely hashbrowns and eggs—well, he pushed this thought firmly to the back of his mind.

Jittery cheap on coffee and sealed with grease, Nylund slapped his coins to the counter and entered the morning all over again. His joints were needly and wired, bending slightly under his weight and springing him forward. He fairly leapt the stairs to the elevated where his dapper mood was dampened, inevitably, by its closed quarters and the grim expressions of the commuters. But the faces of the newspapers shared good news—'Dam Holds!'—a photo of men in business suits and hard hats congratulating each other before a paneled wall.

Nylund watched his toes snap down the elevated steps and across the swept asphalt to the broad stone mien of store. His brown suit hung thin around him, his thin shirt and almond tie speckled with brown like an egg, and he shot himself like an arrow into the revolving heart of the store.

It was not done for employees to ride the public elevator through the building but Nylund did now, watching the childish thick arrow list like a ship over the numbered halfmoon over the grilled door. It reminded Nylund of time lapse photographies, the moon and stars slipping over the sky at night, but this celestial object, the golden arrow that flies by day, moved backwards, stalled and started before leaping forward again or diving back. Like a spooked horse, Nylund thought again, his third metaphor of the morning.

He rode inside the golden cage behind arrow after seizing arrow until he arrived at Home Furnishings. He was greeted with a familiar screech that seemed to come from the heavily carved dark eagle holding in its claw an incandescent lightbulb on the sconce display opposite. "Nyluuund!"

Nylund ducked out of the celestially lit closet and into the dark hall. Eventually he picked out the Superior who was posing slimly among a display of umbrella stands and hat racks, his gloved hand pausing on the polished handle of one prop umbrella. "It's the Neww Masculinity!" he said, improbably, tilting the umbrella like a dandy and pointing out at Nylund one knifeblade toe.

"Really, in your incredible absence all has gone to sugar around here." He stepped down off the dais. "Not to mention that I covered for you all week with the threadbare suits who came calling. I claimed you'd caught an aristocratic flu on your last safari and were being quarantined for the week. So that's your story!" he said happily, looking at Nylund as if with this outlandish concoction he had presented him with a gift.

Which he had.

"Thanks, sir."

"Anyway, Nylund. Your little misgivings, it turned out, were correct. Our murders-in-the-home display, which we worked on so pain-stakingly, Nylund, was up less than a day before the powers that bzzz bzzz bzzz demanded it taken down lest both of us find ourselves out on our nimble thimbles."

"Sorry to hear that."

"Nylund, might I point out three things."

He paused, waiting for a response. In conversation with the Superior, either nothing was rhetorical or everything was.

"Firstly and secondly, both your elocution, and I may say your bearing have improved dramatically since last we met. Your suit, of course, can't be helped, though you might think of using your employee discount to make some headway in that department."

"Thanks, sir."

"Thirdly and ultimately, you might notice that I have not asked you one word about your whereabouts in the past week. Not one word, Nylund! I do not pry." He paused. "But if you would like to reVEAL to me Nylund, at any time in the future even un petit détail, I would be pleased to know."

"Well," Nylund began, but the Superior raised his umbrella like a baton, knocking down the stand.

"No, Nylund! Nothing at this time. We should treasure our secrets for their brief lives, as we do our own."

There came a dull silence here; the Superior gazed off vaguely as if studying his reflection in a smudged mirror. Then, indeed, he crossed to behind Nylund and wiped at a mirror with a chamois he produced from about his person. The mirror was ringed in heavy oak leaves.

"The New Masculinity, sir," Nylund prompted him.

"Riight Nyluuund! The New Masculinity is our next theme, assigned to us from someone high above us breathing the whiskey air. As an artist, Nylund, I feel some pique at having my subject *assigned*, Nyluuund, but as an artist, also, I am already inspired by it, I can't help myself. We need to move up all the desks, armchairs, liquor safes, cabinets of all measures, spittoons, pelts, humidors and ashtrays. And mirrors, Nylund, mirrors! A series of dens and offices, and the twain shall decidedly meet."

And so Nylund and the Superior set about assembling an exact model of what they imagined controlled them, the rafts of executives and managers oaring about, two floors above.

# CHAPTER 20

The pierced man on every wall was transfixing but you couldn't meet his gaze, it was always upwards if his eyes were open. The flag lay down thinly, like it was missing a vitamin, though this was the second-most important part of the room. Nylund liked the honeycomb speakers over the doorway which could change the fate of the day with their interruptions, though never on his behalf. The curriculum was similar here to that at Nylund's old school, but here they were at a different part of it—ahead in the history, behind in the math. In biology class, the teacher lectured on concepts Nylund felt he had always known, facts that were old to him as his bones themselves, which were not hard through and through but clutched in themselves a spongy layer with remarkable and little known curative qualities which could also become a little hamlet of disease. And his skin was no solid thing, full of drinking holes. Nylund kept his old textbooks stacked under his bed. He sometimes pulled them out to hold them in his lap, but never opened them, not since the long day at the minimart when he turned and turned their pages, waiting for Daisy who never returned.

"Hey froggy, you fourteen?" one of the boys asked one night. He had straw colored hair, skin, and eyes barely darker.

Nylund nodded.

"Look twelve, not even."

"You must be retarded."

Was it true? Nylund kept his head down and didn't reply. He was rewarded with a few slaps on the neck, but luckily his roommates' indecision about whether to call him 'Froggy' or 'Retard' kept a unified front from forming against him. Anyway, everyone in this room probably had something wrong with him, Nylund thought. Everyone was probably at least bad if not also retarded.

One windy day blew her image down to him, the students struggling to keep their red balls on the plane of the asphalt playlot. He stood tilted up against the chainlink, facing inward, trying to will himself through it though also not sure where he would go. He closed his eyes. A little heat nursed through the wind to his cheeks. His light brown hair was cut in bangs around his face and ears, like he was wearing a helmet, and the diamonds from the fence pressed into his head and the back of his ears. His glasses were pushed wrong so he opened his eyes. From the corner, he caught sight of her and flipped around. She was down on the corner at the end of the street. She was wearing a shiny purple puffy jacket he had never seen before, her stringy hair was long against her back and picked up in the wind and flew around like always, she looked the same, what had she been doing? She lifted her hand to shield her eyes and looked up the street, not towards Nylund, but across the way from him. "Daisy!" he shrieked. If she heard him in the wind she would have stopped and run to him but she walked off the opposite way so she must not have heard.

\*

115

Nylund walked away from the huge gold-lit department store with the key banging against his chest. Something banging from the outside, and something banging from the inside. Met at no rhythm. They made a noise; his ear was full of it. Science class: pencil sketch: noise was raw before humans applied technology to it, marked it and boxed it up. He sidled into the solid steam of the diner. Everyone was in place: paper cap on the counter-man, tilted like light's collection plate, green properties of the dress of the lonely woman. Thick gold chain. She was sealed in her orbit. The man slapped down water in an amber plastic cup that made light go thick inside it and let no light through. Red heat lamps eyed the food but cast no warmth beyond the counter and into the room. The room had its own field of warmth: a dirty, soapy element. Dishwater. The laminated menus creaked in their stands. Parsley shone a glowing green on the hull of a plate going by. It caught and cut his eye as if it had just been invented. Nylund took the key from around his neck and placed it on the counter-top; the water-stained ceiling groaned and moved closer. The gold-whorled linoleum clicked and he memorized how the key looked: normal, a light brown, its grooved flank and separable teeth like a series of clicks like a handful of pills in the palm that made the tumblers fall down and the lock fall open like a hot-lit circus tent. What lock, what lock. He played it backwards. Click, click. At his feet, the Grandson's million filaments chopped away. He slunk away like a dog. Click: klieglights. Premier lights. Morpheus, click. Clocks. Blotting paper. Salt on fire. Ingushetia. A serpent made of concrete: manmade, mythological fauna. A clicking cockroach coat. The movie magazine's defunct theology both technology and biology—stacked and closed. The rat novel and the firey masthead. Click: the showercurtain game. The water giggle. Clumped mirrory nymphs. Screens. Steve McQueen above the tetanus. The green ribbon pulling tighter till it popped. The vanity, tied, ivying. Diving, stealing. Driving, stealing space. Sliding on bare bones: ankles, sneakers. Clicked by on thought: machines and capsules. Conquistadors in their portable empire machine. Zip home in their cleft helmets: unzipper the sky at the cranial ridge, the peak, Helena, Montana, Darien, Connecticut. The slit that splits and holds. Rowed teeth: cleave. The closet slump. Click of raked, tilting wires, a city's signals, cacophonous clicks. In the counter's condensation, the bill lies bleeding. Carbon, lint. The key before him. The moment before the surface swallows it up.

*

He sees a bridge against slate-gray water. He's up in the air. Wind in the small of his back where his jacket rides up. The bridge is built from cables and chords. It's a showplace, a shoelace. It's an experiment. Footfalls synchronize, and then the bridge begins to wave. Winds off the lakeshore. Fireflies winking at each other across a meadow like a rec room carpet. Dense, synthetic green. The first wave of the epidemic lifts its fist in the air. Patterns: a firefly winking inside it. On the graph like a butterfly net, the epidemic relaxes and spreads out. It gets comfortable in the landscape: it 'makes itself.' Night slides in like a shelf, turns the city vertical. The buildings shift from face to sharp. He lies down on this carpet like a holy man. Eye to eye with a high-rise office where the plastic bins bear sunny hazard stamps. Camera: the dark room in his eye. Far up North, in the small end of the needle, the knight takes off his mylar anorak and lays it down amid the glittery muck. The skibooted maiden minces across it. Her visor blocks out her eyes. Nylund's on his feet at a clearing in the woods. There is a log with life underneath. If he kicks the log, he exposes the life. Will it burn up or burrow deeper. There is an object in his coat; it's slipped from the pocket to the lining. Under his arm, a book with a gummed fraying corner, you can see the cardboard inside. The knights look bored under their coloring book standards. His fingers read the spine. He hears footfalls behind him. And then before him Daisy arrives, orange hair splayed out against her purple collar, a light from behind, a new gold purse swinging and glinting in its beats, in and out of view. He steps over the log, he crosses the clearing. He leans forward in slow motion and the book drops from his crooked arm to her feet. He reaches through his pocket and grabs for the stub end of the object. He brings it slowly out. She raises her palm as he points it right at her. The sunlight lights up the blood in her fingers. He pushes the key into her hand.

# ACKNOWLEDGMENTS

Excerpts from *Nylund, the Sarcographer* appeared in *H_NGM_N*, *Typo Magazine*, *Fairy Tale Review*, */nor*, *Moonlit*, *2nd Avenue Poetry*, and *Tarpaulin Sky*.

The author would also like to express extreme gratitude to Kate Bernheimer for her help in the revision and assembly of this book.

# ABOUT THE AUTHOR

Joyelle McSweeney is the author of *The Red Bird* and *The Commandrine and Other Poems*, both from Fence. She is a co-founder and co-editor of Action Books and *Action, Yes*, a press and web quarterly for international writing and hybrid forms. She writes regular reviews for *Rain Taxi*, *The Constant Critic*, and other venues and teaches in the MFA Program at Notre Dame. Her next book will be the science fiction novel *Flet*, forthcoming from Fence in 2008.

# TARPAULIN SKY PRESS
## CURRENT AND FORTHCOMING TITLES

*[one love affair]\**, by Jenny Boully
Perfectbound & handbound editions

*Body Language*, by Mark Cunningham
Perfectbound & handbound editions

*Attempts at a Life*, by Danielle Dutton
Perfectbound & handbound editions

*32 Pedals and 47 Stops*, by Sandy Florian
Chapbook

*Figures for a Darkroom Voice*,
by Noah Eli Gordon and Joshua Marie Wilkinson,
with images by Noah Saterstrom
Perfectbound & handbound editions

*Nylund, the Sarcographer*, by Joyelle McSweeney
Perfectbound & handbound editions

*Give Up*, by Andrew Michael Roberts
Chapbook

*A Mirror to Shatter the Hammer*, by Chad Sweeney
Chapbook

*The Pictures*, by Max Winter
Perfectbound & handbound editions

## www.tarpaulinsky.com